PLEASE WRITE BACK!

To Charlie
—J.M.

Text and illustrations copyright © 2010 by Jennifer E. Morris.

All rights reserved. Published by Scholastic Inc.
SCHOLASTIC, CARTWHEEL BOOKS, and associated logos
are trademarks and/or registered trademarks of Scholastic Inc.
Lexile is a registered trademark of MetaMetrics, Inc.

Library of Congress Cataloging-in-Publication Data

Morris, J. E. (Jennifer E.)
Please write back! / by Jennifer E. Morris.
p. cm. -- (Scholastic reader. Level 1)
Summary: Alfie writes a letter to his grandmother and eagerly
awaits her reply.
ISBN-13: 978-0-545-11506-3 (pbk. : alk. paper)
ISBN-10: 0-545-11506-X (pbk. : alk. paper)
[1. Letters--Fiction. 2. Grandmothers--Fiction.] I. Title. II. Series.

PZ7.M82824Ple 2010
[E]--dc22   2009011176

ISBN: 978-0-545-11506-3

Printed in the U.S.A. 40 • First printing, April 2010

PLEASE WRITE BACK!

by Jennifer E. Morris

SCHOLASTIC INC.

Alfie wrote a letter to Grandma.

Dear Grandma

Alfie addressed the letter.

First Class

Grandma
276 Everglade Trail
Sw___ ____ville, FL 00495

He stamped the letter.

And he mailed the letter.

Then he waited for Grandma to write back.

He waited the next day.

And the next day.

And the next day.

But Grandma's letter
did not come.

The next day, Alfie
did not wait for the mail.

"Are you Alfie?" asked
the mailman.

"Do you have a letter for me?" asked Alfie.

"No," said the mailman.

"I have a box."

Inside was a letter.

And a big batch of cookies! Hooray!

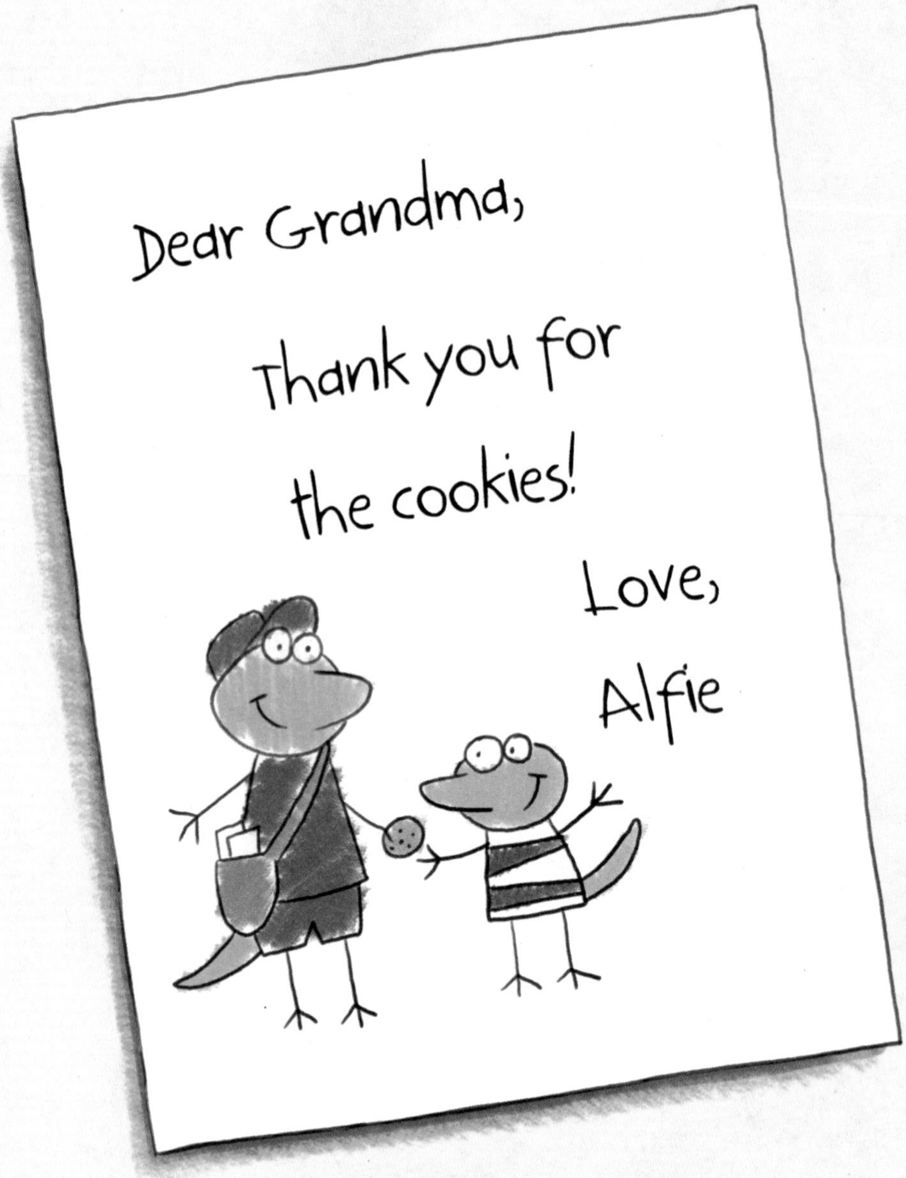
Dear Grandma,
Thank you for
the cookies!
Love,
Alfie